Adapted by Jane B. Mason

Based on the motion picture written by Jonathan Betuel

THEODORE REX

SCHOLASTIC INC.

New York   Toronto   London   Auckland   Sydney

ISBN 0-590-67784-5

Photo Credits
All interior photos Suzanne Hanover
Cover and title page photos of Theodore Rex by Blake Little
Cover photo of Whoopi Goldberg by Suzanne Hanover

12 11 10 9 8 7 6 5 4 3 2 1   5 6 7 8 9/9 0/0

Printed in the U.S.A.   24

First Scholastic Printing, December 1995

Theodore Rex leaned back in his recliner chair and sighed happily. After a busy day at work, a little nap was just what he needed.

But soon after he fell asleep, Teddy awoke with a strong feeling of dread. Something terrible was happening to a fellow dinosaur!

Teddy sat up and reached for the holophone. "This is Teddy Rex," he told Grid Police Headquarters. "I had a flash."

The police told Teddy that a dinosaur had been murdered.

Teddy frowned. It was the first dinosaur murder since the prehistoric beasts had been brought back to life. Why would anyone want to kill a dinosaur?

Teddy had to find out.

Not far away, a lot of important people were at a fancy party for the New Eden Foundation. Its founder, Elizar Kane, would be making an important speech.

Teddy knew that the police commissioner was at the party, and he needed to speak with him right away. He hopped into his Rex Cruiser and drove across town.

At the door, Teddy flashed his police department badge. But on his way into the room — *WHAM!* — he banged his head on the top of the door frame. Rubbing his head, Teddy stepped forward. It wasn't easy being eight feet tall!

Commissioner Lynch was talking to a co-worker named Alex Summers. Teddy stepped forward. "Commissioner Lynch," he said. "There's been a dinocide, and I'd like to be assigned to the case."

Lynch and Summers stared at Teddy in surprise. He was a police department tour guide, *not* a detective. But then Summers got a funny look in his eyes. He pulled Lynch aside.

"When news gets out," Summers said, "we could have riots between dinosaurs and humans." He looked over at Teddy, who was munching away on a clawful of cookies. "Our shiny prince over there could make *both* of us look good."

"The case is yours," Lynch told Teddy a minute later. "We'll be teaming you up with a pro."

Across town, police officer Katie Coltrane was getting home after a hard day's work. She was tired and her feet hurt. Being a cop in the Grid wasn't easy.

BEEP! BEEP! Her beeper went off. "Report to the Explorer's Club," a voice said. "The commissioner wants to see you."

A few minutes later, Katie arrived at the club. "There's been a crime, and your name came up," Summers said.

"Actually, it's a dinocide," Teddy explained.

"Teddy Rex, meet Katie Coltrane," Commissioner Lynch put in. "You two solve this case together."

Katie's jaw dropped. She had nothing against dinosaurs, but Teddy was a tour guide! Working with him would definitely ruin her reputation.

"This is not a request," Lynch added.

Katie frowned. Like it or not, she'd be teaming up with an eight-foot prehistoric beast.

Later that night, Elizar Kane rode home in his limousine. Cars were not allowed in the Grid, but Elizar Kane was special. He had a lot of money. He had re-created dinosaurs. And he had made the Grid a better, safer place.

At least that's what he wanted people to think. The truth was, Elizar Kane didn't care about dinosaurs or people. He just wanted power — and would do anything to get it.

Across the Grid, Teddy and Katie were in the dinosaur lab at the Natural History Museum. Teddy was doing some serious sleuthing. He shined a light into the wound on the victim's snout and pulled out a small metal object.

Next, he took a tail print. "The scale patterns on our tails are all different," he explained.

Teddy faxed the print to his computer. It identified the victim as Oliver Rex, who'd lived with Molly Rex at 35 Prehistoric Place. They had their first lead!

The detectives headed over to the nightclub where Molly worked as a singer. Soon they were in her dressing room.

Teddy couldn't take his eyes off Molly. She was so beautiful!

"Grid police," Katie said gruffly.

Teddy frowned. Why was Katie so mean?

"You catch more bees with honey," Molly crooned.

"We're after a killer, not bees, *honey*," Katie replied. "The murderer of Oliver Rex."

Molly nearly fainted from shock, and Teddy's heart went out to her.

"What did he do?" Katie asked, sounding as gruff as ever.

"Oliver worked for New Eden," Molly answered.

Katie tapped her chin in thought. New Eden seemed like a good place to ask questions.

After talking to Molly for a few more minutes, Teddy handed her his card and asked her to call him if she thought of anything else.

Teddy gave Molly a sad smile. "I feel for you," he said softly.

"How sweet," Molly replied. "Why don't you come to Oliver's service tomorrow, Mr. Rex?"

"Call me Teddy," Teddy said.

Molly smiled. "My friends call me Molly."

Katie rolled her eyes. Dinos were so mushy! "Mine call me *collect*," she said.

After thanking Molly, the detectives went their separate ways for the night.

The next morning, Teddy and Katie set off for the New Eden compound. But on the way they stopped to watch some kids play street hockey. One of the kids was Sebastian, a friend of Katie's.

They hung out for a while, and Teddy impressed everyone with his tail-shooting ability. He scored six goals in five seconds!

But from a nearby garbage can, somebody was watching . . . somebody who wanted Katie and Teddy out of the way.

Later, at the New Eden compound, the detectives headed for Kane's office.

"We're investigating a dinocide," Teddy told Mr. Kane. "And it seems that Oliver Rex worked here."

Kane looked shocked. "He worked in Species Data," he said. "That's where we keep track of vanishing life-forms."

"Did Oliver have any enemies that you knew of?" Teddy asked.

Kane shook his head. "I can't imagine him making a single enemy."

"It only takes one," Katie reminded him.

Kane's face was grim. "Oliver's death was tragic," he said sadly. "I'm sorry I can't be of more help to you."

After the detectives left, Kane sat down in his chair. "This is getting out of hand," he said nervously.

He called in his right-hand man, Edge. Edge knew just what to do.

A little while later, Sebastian was blading down an alley when he saw a kid playing a video game. But when he stepped up to play the game himself, he realized it was attached to the back of a truck.

"Hey!" Sebastian protested. Someone was slapping handcuffs on him. The next thing he knew, he was dragged into the truck as it sped away.

The next stop for Katie and Teddy was Oliver's funeral. Afterward, Teddy invited Molly over for some homemade macadamia chip cookies.

"How can I say no to a Rex who bakes cookies from scratch?" Molly crooned.

By the time night fell, Teddy and Molly were dancing a mad tango — and falling in love.

But someone was watching them from the roof of the building across the street. And he had plans for Molly Rex. . . .

Later that night, Teddy and Katie were called to Gun Command. An officer had run some tests on the object Teddy had found in the dinosaur victim's snout.

"It's a metal butterfly that carries an explosive device," the officer said. "The work of a man called the Toymaker."

Teddy and Katie found the Toymaker in his shop. But when they started to question him, he disappeared down a floor chute.

A second later — *BOOM!* — a loud explosion knocked Katie off her feet. "I'm okay," she said weakly. "But that little slug got away."

Teddy grinned. He'd caught the Toymaker with his tail! He lifted him into the air threateningly.

All of a sudden, the Toymaker was telling the detectives what they wanted to know. "Kane controls everything . . . he's kidnapped Sebastian . . . he's at the compound. . . ."

Minutes later, the detectives arrived at the New Eden compound. The truck broke through the gate, and Katie stepped on the gas. *CRASH!* — it smashed through the wall of Kane's office, taking Kane by surprise.

"Where's Sebastian?" Katie demanded.

"Locked up in the zoo, where he belongs," Kane said.

"Keep an eye on him," Katie told Teddy. "I'm going to find Sebastian."

"You're under arrest," Teddy told Kane when they were alone.

Kane laughed, and the walls around them slid away.

Teddy gasped. Kane had nuclear missiles — enough to destroy the whole world!

"I have no room for humans in my new world," Kane said. "Soon they won't ever trouble me again." He pushed a remote-control button, and the missiles were activated.

"No!" Teddy cried. In a flash, he swung his tail in a sweeping arc, knocking Kane off his feet.

Meanwhile, Katie had found Sebastian. "Hi, kid," she said, opening his cage. "How you doing?"

Sebastian smiled up at her. "I've been worse," he said.

Katie took his hand. "Come on," she said. "We've got to get back to Kane's office."

In Kane's office, Teddy found Molly in a chamber. He pounded on the glass wall. But she didn't wake up.

"No!" he cried, letting out a howl.

Molly stirred and opened her eyes. "Theo?" she said softly.

Teddy sighed in relief. She was all right!

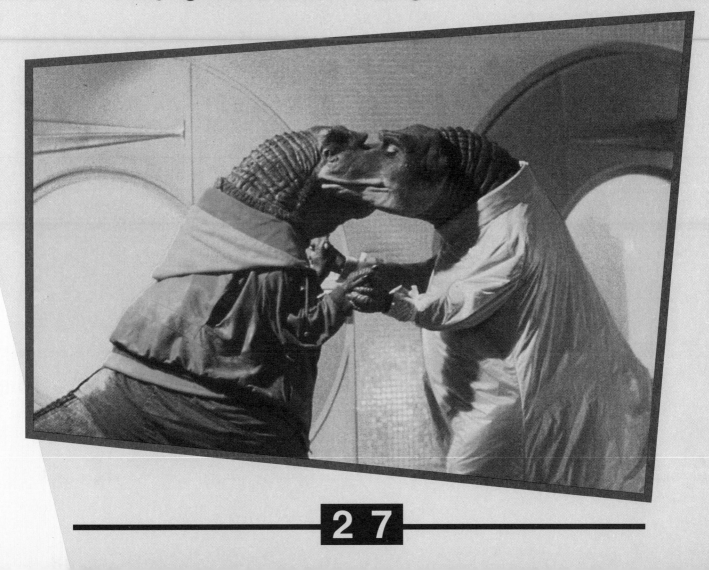

Katie and Sebastian made it back to the office in record time. But the missiles were going to fire at any moment, and Kane had disappeared with the remote control.

Teddy raced out the door, hot on Kane's heels. But Kane saw him coming and fired a shot. . . .

Teddy fell to the sidewalk in a heap.

"You must learn to accept defeat." Kane stood over Teddy.

"You're under arrest," Teddy said weakly.

Kane laughed and walked away. He climbed into a New Eden car. Starting it up, he headed straight for Teddy!

Teddy reached out and wrapped his tail around a tree trunk. Summoning his last bit of strength, he pulled as hard as he could. A second later the car whizzed by, missing him by inches.

Teddy jumped to his feet and fired his gun. Out shot a rope with a hook on the end. The hook latched onto Kane's coat and Teddy reeled him in as if he were a big fish.

Teddy grabbed the remote control from Kane's pocket and pressed the abort button.

Everyone was safe!

Several days later, a crowd gathered at the recently opened New Eden Zoo to honor Katie and Teddy.

"Theodore Rex, it's my honor to promote you to Detective, First Class," Commissioner Lynch said. "And Katie Coltrane," he went on, "you have officially been transferred to the Public Relations Department."

The crowd cheered, and Molly and Sebastian looked on proudly.
The Grid was safe once again. . . .
Thanks to the strangest and greatest detective team ever!